Disclaimer

This is a work of fiction. Any names, businesses, characters, events, incidents and places are either the product of the author's imagination or used in a fictitious manner. Any resemblance to actual people, living or dead, or actual events or occurrences is purely coincidental.

Tagged

By Alessandra Bancroft
Copyright © 2015

Table of Contents

Chapter 1: Moonlight and a Dark Alley

Lea pressed her back against the building, the rough bricks pushing painfully into the exposed skin of her shoulder blades. She fought to breathe, but the summer air was so heavy with humidity that it felt as though her lungs couldn't draw it in past the frantic pounding of her heart. Footsteps thudded on the uneven pavement and reverberated through the alley. Lea felt the panic creeping further up her throat, and the tears stinging the corners of her eyes. She willed them not to fall. It always made things worse when she cried.

Stepping carefully out of the shadow where she had been hiding, Lea started to run. Behind her, the footsteps grew louder and faster as Brent chased her, screaming her name through a haze of cheap beer and frustration. The end of the alley seemed to stretch further and further from her as she ran, ankles struggling to keep her balanced as the spike heels of her shoes caught in the breaks and dips in the pavement.

She was only a few yards from the end of the alley and the road that waited beyond. She hadn't even thought about what she would do when she got there. If she could just get out of the alley, maybe then she had a chance.

Gasping for air, she pushed forward a few more steps, then sobbed as she felt Brent's hand grasp the back of her hair and yank her roughly off her feet. Lea stumbled to the ground, landing hard on her hip. She yelped at the pain of Brent pulling her hair, which just made him pull harder. Slithering against the ground trying to get free, she felt tiny bits of loose gravel cutting into her palms and scratching her legs.

"Brent, please," she sobbed.

"Shut up, bitch," he snarled, and she felt the blinding explosion of his fist against her cheekbone.

This was by far not the first time their fights had escalated to this point, but that did not lessen the pain, the horror, or the humiliation as she lay on the ground, finally free of his grip on her hair but unable to move. Brent's hands came to her shoulders and forced her onto her back. Lea tried to scream, but the sound died under his hands. His knee dug into her stomach to pin her to the ground as he stared down at her. The fire in his eyes was all too familiar. There was brutality there, cruelty that stemmed from long before she met him and that would likely continue long after she was gone.

Brent leaned down to kiss her and Lea twisted away from him, knowing it would likely make him even angrier but not able to stomach the taste of his sour, disgusting mouth. She caught a fleeting glimpse of the road beyond the end of the alley and the slice of moonlight illuminating it before she felt Brent's hand thrust roughly up her skirt. His other hand grabbed her neck and helplessness washed over her. The way he clutched her neck right beneath her jaw made it so that she couldn't even move her head. She could only lay there as Brent tore her panties from her body.

The smile on Brent's face made her stomach turn. It was a smile she had seen so many times before but that never failed to make her tremble with fear. She knew not to close her eyes, not to cry. She tried to focus on the moonlight rather than the sound of him fumbling with his belt buckle.

Suddenly the moonlight disappeared as a shadow fell across her. The weight on her stomach and the pressure on her neck eased as someone lifted Brent off of her and tossed him roughly onto the ground several feet away. Lea scrambled to her feet, watching as a tall, broad-shouldered man landed a kick directly into Brent's face. Blood splattered against his skin and Brent wailed, curling in on himself. Dressed entirely in black, the man looked like one of the shadows spread across the alley as he lifted Brent off the ground with another kick to his stomach.

Brent tried to stand, but the man kicked him again, forcing him back to the ground. Lea screamed, finally able to find her voice. Her hand flew to her mouth and she stumbled back several steps.

"I told you to shut up," Brent growled as he started to stagger to his feet.

Blood trickled down his lips and into his mouth, and Lea's stomach turned as he spit some of it toward her. He gave another of his lecherous sneers a second before the mysterious man's fist made contact with his face and Brent crumpled to the ground again.

"Don't talk to her," he said, his voice low and gravelly, but controlled.

Lea waited for Brent to get up, but he didn't. He remained a contorted mess on the pavement, the shallow rise and fall of his shoulder the only thing that told Lea he was still alive. The man turned and took a step toward her. Intense blue eyes stared at her from under a shock of nearly-black hair and she felt her breath catch.

"Are you alright?" he asked.

Lea couldn't respond. She couldn't find the words. All she could do was take a few steps back, turn, and run toward the end of the alley and the moonlit street that waited beyond.

When she turned the corner onto the street, the air suddenly felt cooler and less oppressive. She paused to lean her back against the smooth metal of one of the garage doors that lined the street and slid down until she sat on the sidewalk. The tears finally began to stream down her face, washing away some of the dirt that had gathered as she struggled. In the distance, Lea heard the wail of a police siren swelling over the night sounds of the city around her. She waited until they were almost unbearably loud and joined by the crunching of tires skidding into the other side of the alley before she stood.

She straightened her skirt, wiped a smear of blood from her shoulder, and turned back into the alley. Her eyes fell on the dark stranger helping a police officer pull Brent from the ground. Another officer grabbed the stranger from behind, struggling with him as if trying to put him in handcuffs. She didn't remember speaking, but she must have, because all of them turned to look at her. Lea walked forward deliberately, staring straight at Brent without fear twisting in her chest. For the first time, she didn't need to run.

Chapter 2: Out of the Shadows

Darkness fell again and still Lea didn't feel afraid. Her body stretched languidly against the sheets of her bed, reveling in the cool, empty place beside her, appreciating the comfort of moving how she pleased. The ache in her cheekbone was beginning to fade and, along with it, the heaviness that had filled her for so long. In its place was a new feeling, one of curiosity and desire.

She had only gotten a brief glimpse at the stranger's face in the alley, but those few moments were enough to register that he was breathtaking. The intensity of his eyes sent shivers down her spine even as they looked back at her through her memory, and Lea found herself longing to look at them again. In the few days following Brent's arrest, she had been so busy dealing with the police, packing everything in her apartment, and moving across the city that she barely remembered that she had not thanked the stranger for stepping in and rescuing her. As soon as she convinced the police that he had not hurt her, but in fact had saved her, they let him go. He walked away, melting into the shadows, before she could say anything to him.

Now she could not stop thinking about him. She replayed those few minutes in her mind again and again, carefully editing out Brent and focusing on the stranger. Beneath his black clothing she imagined a body as chiseled and perfect as his face, muscles rippling beneath smooth skin embedded with sleek black ink. She wondered what his tattoos might be and where she could discover them.

On the fourth night, she couldn't stand just thinking about him anymore. She wanted to see him one more time, to thank him for what he did for her, to hear his voice again. Carefully covering the slowly-disappearing bruise on her cheek with makeup, she left her new apartment and headed back to the dark alley. Nerves made her stomach tremble, but she had difficulty discerning how much of that was because of what she remembered about her last time in that alley and how much was the butterflies that appeared when she thought of seeing the stranger again.

A rare fog settled over the city, creating a mist that rolled through the alley, accentuating the shadows and making it difficult for Lea to see in front of her. Light from two lampposts positioned on either end of the alley created an eerie glow that intensified her nerves as she walked carefully down the uneven pavement. This time she was wearing flats and felt more stable walking along the broken segments.

Around her, the alley was still as if the fog was muffling any sound from the nearby restaurants. Her footsteps sounded loud in her ears and, after a few moments, she was aware of another set joining hers. They pounded in syncopation as she walked. A chill slipped down her spine as she felt eyes on her back. Pausing in the middle of the alley, Lea turned and stared through the fog in the direction of the footsteps.

A dark figure stopped ten feet from her. The fog swirled around him, climbing across his black clothing as if caressing him. Lea's breath caught as he took another step forward and she saw his haunting blue eyes piercing through the darkness toward her.

"Hi," she said timidly.

The stranger hesitated for a few seconds and then strode forward. He dug his hands into the pockets of his hooded long-sleeve t-shirt, leaving his throat and his face the only exposed skin. Lea felt a strange compulsion to touch her fingertips to the dip at the base of his throat.

"Hey," he responded, confusion and apprehension evident in his tone as he approached her, "what are you doing here?"

There was an awkward silence between them as Lea tried to find the right words to explain why she was in the alley again. Finally, she decided there was no reason to make up excuses.

"I was hoping to find you. I wanted to say thank you for what you did the other night."

The stranger stiffened slightly, squaring his shoulders against gratitude as if he wasn't used to having people speak kindly to him.

"It wasn't anything more than anyone would do."

"I know for a fact that that isn't true. You are the first person to ever protect me from Brent. I just wanted you to know how much I appreciate it."

"Are you alright?"

Those had been the first words he had ever said to her and they sent a new shiver through her when she heard them again.

"I'm getting there."

The stranger nodded and started to walk around her on his way toward the other end of the alley. Disappointment settled into Lea's belly as she watched him walk away from her.

"Wait. What's your name?"

He didn't turn as he continued into the fog.

"Jordan," he called back.

"I'm Lea."

Jordan turned so that he walked backwards for a few steps.

"Hello, Lea," he said, turning his back and walking the rest of the way down the alley and disappearing between two buildings near the end.

Two days later Lea was ready to get back to work. Her barely-begun project waited for her on her kitchen table, one of the few things that she had actually unpacked since her hurried move. Gripping a mug of coffee, Lea dropped down into one of the white wooden chairs at the edge of the table and reached out to pick up one sheet of paper. It was a printout of a picture she had taken of a word spray painted in bright pink across a concrete wall. The rest of the photos spread across the table featured variations of that tag in different colors on different walls, as well as a few other tags and a large mural.

Her career as a photojournalist gave her the opportunity to explore things that fascinated her and create stories about them. Although Lea spent most of her career doing fairly soft, safe stories such as following brides planning their weddings or telling the histories of up-and-coming chefs, a few months ago she had come up with an edgier story that would push her out of her comfort zone and into a world that had always fascinated her.

Lea planned to investigate graffiti throughout the city, exploring the different styles and comparing them. She hoped that if the editor liked this story she would be able to travel to different cities to repeat it. In order to do that, however, she needed to get this one finished and her deadline was looming. She gulped down the last of her coffee and headed to her bedroom to dress and get ready for the adventure she had planned for that afternoon.

A few hours later she walked carefully along a narrow passage beneath a bridge that crossed the massive river surrounding the city. Above her, she could hear the rumble of an impending train that would soon cross the bridge on its way back to the train yard. She pressed her hand to the concrete support on one side of the passage, waiting as the sound grew louder and then shook through her as the train passed directly overhead.

"The concrete makes it sound louder," a voice said from behind her when the roar finally faded into the distance.

Lea nearly dropped her camera as she spun around to face Jordan. He stood just outside of the shade created by the bridge, one hand gripping the strap of a black bag slung over his shoulder. Despite the warmth, he was wearing another loose long-sleeved shirt over black jeans. Lea felt an involuntary whimper escape her lips and hoped he didn't notice.

"Jordan," she said, her voice coming out as more of a sigh than the greeting she had intended. She looked down at her camera, pretending to adjust the setting as she tried to sound more casual, "What are you doing here?"

Jordan let out a dry chuckle and started toward her. "It seems we ask each other that question a lot."

Lea smiled at him. "I guess we do."

"This is one of my favorite places to come and," he seemed to hesitate, testing words in his mind until he found the right one, "think. So..." he paused.

"What am I doing here?" she asked.

They both laughed and Lea felt the warmth of attraction blended with happiness creeping up through her body.

"Yeah."

"I'm working."

Jordan cocked his head at her and she showed him her camera.

"I'm a photojournalist. I'm working on a project about the graffiti throughout the city."

Interest flickered across Jordan's face. "Oh, really?" he asked, stepping closer to her, "why did you pick that topic?"

Lea shrugged and started scanning through the pictures she had already captured on her camera." It fascinates me."

"What fascinates you about it?"

Jordan's voice was lower now and he was standing close enough beside her that Lea could feel his breath touching her cheek. The closeness brought the butterflies back and she felt her heartbeat quicken.

Chapter 3: Whispering Into the Past

Lea stepped away from Jordan so she could point out one of the elaborate tags on the concrete bridge support.

"I love the colors and the different styles." She traced the jagged edges of a tag left by the same tagger she had focused most of her project around with a finger. "It's beautiful."

Her voice dropped lower as if she were speaking directly to the paint and the artist behind it. She reached higher to touch another piece and Jordan's hand wrapped around her arm, gently pulling it down away from the wall.

"My god," he said and even though she wouldn't look at him, she could feel his eyes scanning the edges of the bruise that came up over the side of her arm.

Lea tried to take her arm away from his grip, but Jordan held it still, turning it over to examine the mottled color that spread along the underside of her wrist and the inside of her arm. She hadn't expected to encounter anyone while out taking more pictures so she had done nothing to cover the bruise. Embarrassment burned across her cheeks and she looked away.

"I'm fine," she said, finally slipping her arm out of Jordan's grasp and bringing it up against her body to conceal it.

"Yeah, I'm sure. How many times have you said that?"

Lea sat down on the worn gravel path, suddenly feeling tired and overwhelmed. She rested her head back against the concrete support and let her eyes drift closed. Beside her she felt Jordan lower himself to sit beside her. He wasn't close enough that they actually touched, but she could sense the warmth radiating from him only inches away. They sat in silence for a few long seconds, listening together to the wind as it caught under the bridge, amplifying its sound.

"Why did you stay?" he asked finally.

The question was so personal it took Lea off guard. It was one she had asked herself countless times before, but coming from this man, this beautiful, mysterious stranger, it seemed to carry much more weight. She opened her eyes and saw him looking at her.

"I can't be the first person to ask you that," he said.

She shook her head. "You're not. I didn't know what to say to them, either."

"How long were you with him?"

"Three years."

"Did he always hurt you?"

The question hit Lea hard. A sharp pain went through her as her heart constricted.

"No," she said, forcing herself to think back, sift through the dark memories to find the ones from the beginning, before his anger had taken over. "We were really happy for the first year. Then things got rocky. Then they got really rocky. It was the worst a few weeks before...before you saved me."

"I will never understand," Jordan said, his voice dropped to a growl as he turned to look out over the river.

"Neither will I," she admitted. "I never thought I could defend a man who did that, but then one day I realized I was hiding bruises and making up excuses and trying to explain away his cruelty as a twisted sense of humor. By the end it was almost like I was living someone else's life. I had cut off so much of my emotion that I can only remember the buildup, the terror, and the recovery. There really wasn't anything else. Just that, in cycle."

She should have been embarrassed about revealing all of this to him, but Jordan sparked the same safe, comforted feeling that it had in the alley that first night. He made her feel secure enough that she could say things she had never given voice to before, not even to herself.

"How do so many women let themselves get lost like that? Why is a man who makes you feel that way worth spending even a day with, much less years?"

"It isn't really about what he is worth. After a while, you begin to believe that he is all you are worth."

Lea felt Jordan's hand come gently to the side of her face and turn it until she looked at him.

"Do you really believe that?" he asked.

"I don't know what else to believe."

Her voice was so weak she wasn't even sure he heard her and her eyes lowered. She felt him tilt her face slightly so that she raised her eyes to him again. His thumb slid across the fading hint of bruise on her cheekbone.

"You are beautiful," he said quietly, but insistently. "You are worth far more than that."

The statement felt angry and painful rather than like a compliment and Lea wondered if it wasn't directed just at her.

"Someone else you know?" Lea asked.

Jordan looked away and Lea could see the muscles in his forearm twitching as one hand grasped the other wrist, his arms resting on his bent knees.

"My best friend," he answered softly.

"What happened?"

Emotion swirled through his intense eyes, darkening them as he stared at the rushing grey water. For reasons she did not quite understand, Lea slid slightly closer to him.

"She got mixed up with guy. None of us trusted him, so she got pretty distant from everybody. Even me. He was really good to her at first, at least that's how she talked about him, and then one night we ran into each other and she hugged me. Apparently he didn't like that because he grabbed her by her hair and dragged her away before I could stop him. The next time I saw her, she had bruises all over her arms, and a lot of makeup trying to cover one on her cheek."

"Jordan, I –" Lea started, but paused when he reached into his pocket, pulled out his wallet, and showed her a picture of a dark-haired girl smiling into the camera.

"Wow. She's gorgeous," Lea said, watching as he ran his thumb ran over the picture.

He hastily tucked the picture away and shoved his wallet back into his pocket.

"Yeah, she was. By the time he got through with her, though, we couldn't even have an open casket."

Lea's hand flew to her mouth, nausea nearly overwhelming her.

"Oh my god," she whispered.

Jordan scrambled to his feet. He took several steps away, then turned back and strode toward her with such ferocity Lea pulled back.

"She was my best friend. My best friend from the time I was four years old and I couldn't save her. He killed her and I wasn't there."

Lea could see his body shaking with anger and she stood slowly, controlling her movements so as to not to incite him any further. She walked toward him, reaching up to rest her hands on his shoulders. They felt solid and strong beneath her hands and she stroked them gently.

"It wasn't your fault," she told him softly, forcing her voice past the emotion welling in her throat. "She made her own decision. You couldn't have made it for her."

"I should have protected her."

"It isn't always possible to protect people," she whispered, a tear slipping down her cheek as she realized that by stepping between her and Brent, by saving her, he had tried to save his best friend.

Heat built between them as Lea let her hands continue to glide along his shoulders, dipping further to explore the hard muscles of his upper arms through his thin shirt. He leaned toward her slightly, bringing his mouth down so that his lips nearly brushed her ear.

"Can I trust you?" he whispered.

A shiver rippled from where his breath touched on her ear down through her body and settled between her thighs. Her hands squeezed his arms a little tighter as if to find strength as her knees grew weak.

Chapter 4: Chasing Secrets

It had been a long time since Lea had truly trusted anyone, but she felt safe with Jordan, even more so with his strong arms in her hands, and wanted him to feel safe with her. She nodded breathlessly.

"Yes. You can trust me."

Jordan's hands touched her hips.

"Can I tell you a secret?" he whispered, this time barely grazing her ear with his lips.

She nodded again.

"Yes."

She felt his hands start to move up her body and her heart beat even faster.

"When we were younger, Lisa and I were always together. She said I was her favorite toy." He laughed quietly and ran his hands up to her shoulders, "When we were in middle school she started calling me Tigger."

As he spoke, Jordan's hands traveled down her arms until one wrapped around her wrist again. He took her hand away from his shoulder and turned her gently, guiding her forward a few steps. Lea was suddenly aware that her eyes were closed ad she felt him press her hand to the concrete. His hand stretched over hers briefly and then his touch disappeared as he stepped away from her.

Lea's eyes slid open and she gasped as she saw that her hand was spread across a bright blue and green version of her favorite tag, really noticing for the first time that the four sharp, overlapping letters were "TGGR."

Tears spilled down her cheeks and she stroked the letters, feeling the paint and the pain beneath her fingertips. She turned back around to face Jordan.

"You?" she asked and he nodded.

"She was the only one who ever knew that I was an artist. When she died, her mother buried her wearing a necklace with Tigger on it that she always wore. She said it was to keep me with her. That's when I changed my tag. This is how I keep her with me. This way she can never be forgotten. She is everywhere."

He walked up beside her and touched the tag.

"Did you love her?"

The question was much more painful to ask than Lea imagined and she braced herself for the answer.

"Yes," he turned his head to look at her, "but not in the way that you mean. We never could have been together. We never wanted to be. She and I saw each other through everything. She made me strong. I kept her safe." His hand fell away from the concrete. "At least I tried to."

Lea sighed and ran her hand down his back. It felt warm and damp with sweat.

"Why do you always wear long sleeves?" she asked with a soft laugh in her voice, trying to gently change the subject, hoping to wash the pain from his beautiful eyes. "Aren't you hot?"

Jordan turned the rest of the way around so that he faced her and looked down at his arms as if just remembering that he was wearing the unseasonable shirt. He gave a slight smile.

"This is not exactly a legal hobby. The sleeves make it more difficult to identify me just in case someone sees me."

"What do you mean?"

Jordan pushed the sleeves up past his elbows and held his arms out to her. Just as she had imagined, his golden- tanned skin was covered in an intricate network of tattoos from his wrists as far up his arms as she could see. She bit her bottom lip to prevent her groan of appreciation and touched the bold black designs, letting her fingertips explore the ink embedded deep in his skin. Cupping one arm in her palm, she gently turned it over so she could touch the underside of his wrist, feeling the ridges of his veins pulsing beneath his skin.

He let out a long exhalation as she touched further, drawing her fingertips up the inside of his arm to the soft bend. She followed each line deliberately, feeling the seconds slip past uncounted as she learned the curves of his muscle and discovered the details inked into his skin. He drew closer to her as she touched him, easing gradually nearer with each new line she chose to follow.

"You know," she said softly, "I have probably 30 pictures of your tag spread across my kitchen table right now."

"Really?"

"I guess I have been following you for a few weeks now without knowing it."

"Follow me now," he whispered.

Lea's stomach trembled at his words. Jordan stepped back away from her and reached down to grab his bag from where he had dropped it. He slung the bag over his shoulder and started down the path away from her. The sun was starting to set and the rich golden bands of its last gasp of daylight made him glow as he turned behind the concrete support. Not wanting him to get too far away, she took off after him.

Jordan had reached the steep hill on the other side of the bridge when she caught up with him. She didn't ask where they were going; she simply followed. Somehow she knew that whenever she had the chance, she would follow. He did not demand she come along and expect her to trail behind him. She walked by his side and allowed him to lead her, guide her with the trust she placed in him.

They walked along in silence, the light of the day disappearing around them with each step. He glanced over at her occasionally as he led her through an expanse of trees, and she looked back at him confidently. Finally, they emerged at the edge of a set of train tracks. She assumed these also led to the train yard less than a mile away. A single light attached to the side of a tall wooden post on one side of the tracks sent a hazy yellow glow down on a series of boxcars stopped several yards away from them.

Jordan brought a finger to his lips as if to tell her to stay quiet, but she saw him smile behind the gesture, a hint of playfulness breaking through his dark, hard shell. He picked up his pace as he headed for the boxcars and Lea jogged on the balls of her feet to keep up with him. When they reached the edge of the cars, he tossed his bag to the gravel edging of the tracks and crouched down beside it.

Lea watched in quiet fascination as he pulled out several cans of paint, a silver permanent marker, and a black bandana. Moving as if he had forgotten that she was there, Jordan pulled off his shirt and tucked it into the bag. Her mouth watered when she saw that his tattoos continued up his arms, along his shoulders, and down his back.

Sweat shimmered on his skin and powerful, chiseled muscles shifted and flexed as he folded the bandana into a triangle, positioned it over the bottom half of his face, and tied the ends behind his head. He turned to look over his shoulder at her and his shocking eyes stared at her from over the black cloth. Her body responded to him immediately, delicious pressure building low in her belly.

Jordan approached the side of one of the cars and took the top off of the permanent marker. His hand moved quickly as he sketched the outline of a large piece across the dark red metal. It was not his usual tag and she watched the new shape form under his hand with curiosity. She had forgotten about the camera in her hand, so drawn to his dark beauty, the excitement of his rebellion that all she could do was serve witness to the art pouring from him. Lea carefully sat on the side of the hill as the sun sank below the horizon.

The initial outline complete, he tossed the marker back into the bag and picked up one of the cans. He shook the can a few times before removing the cap, pressing the cloth more firmly to his face with his free hand, and starting to spray the paint onto the car. After a few minutes he replaced the cap and traded that can for another. Suddenly, he paused and lifted his head. Lea stiffened as he pulled the bandana down off of his mouth and looked into the distance as if he heard something.

A crunch behind her made her jump.

"Oh, shit," Jordan muttered, "come here."

He grabbed his bag and the loose can of paint on the ground before running down the row of boxcars to one nearly at the end with a door gaping open. Lea got to her feet as quickly as she could and ran after him, dipping down to scoop his shirt off the gravel. Jordan had already jumped into the open car and reached out to pull her in after him. The force sent them into the corner of the car, his back pressed to the wall and Lea draped on his chest with his arm around her waist.

Chapter 5: Breaking Free

Lea panted against Jordan's chest, adrenaline straining her breath more than the short sprint along the tracks. He placed his finger against his lips again, this time to quiet her, and Lea nodded. She could hear heavy footsteps crunching in the gravel outside. Her heart pounded against Jordan and she felt panic creeping into the back of her mind. Jordan held her closely against his body, turning his head toward the wall of the boxcar as if trying to listen more closely to the impending footsteps.

Suddenly the crunching stopped what sounded like just a few feet from their car. Lea struggled to control her breath, trying to stay as quiet as she possibly could. Being pressed to Jordan's bare chest and stomach was making that difficult. His skin was slick with sweat and smelled like salt, warmth, and musk. The combination made her body feel equally hot and slick and she brought her hips forward slightly to push subtly against his.

The sound of the footsteps started again, but now they moved in the opposite direction. Whoever was outside was apparently satisfied that no one was around, and soon the steps faded completely. Lea let out a sigh of relief and dropped her head forward. It fell into the curve between Jordan's neck and shoulder and she felt him go still. She let the tip of her tongue touch his collarbone, picking up a few droplets of sweat.

"Lea," he whispered.

"Yes?"

"We have to get out of here."

"Oh," she said, her voice high with embarrassment and disappointment.

Jordan took her by her shoulders and held her a few inches away from him so that he could look at her.

"That was either the police or another crew, and you really don't want either one to find us in here."

Lea took a step backwards out of his hands and nodded in agreement.

"Ok. Let's go."

Jordan took his shirt from her and slipped it on over his head before putting his bag over his shoulder and peeking out of the door. He looked either way, then jumped down out of the boxcar. Lea dropped down beside him and they took off running together, following the same path up the hill, through the trees, and down the hill on the other side until they were back beneath the bridge.

Once concealed in deep shadow, Jordan turned and pushed her against the concrete support. Lea gasped at the sudden motion and felt a ripple of fear roll down her spine. The trepidation disappeared, however, when he leaned forward and brushed his face along her neck.

"Now you know my secret," he muttered against her skin.

"Mmmm-hmmmm," she murmured, bringing one hand up to rest on the back of his head so that her fingers dipped into his thick ebony hair.

"What's yours?"

She was taken aback by his question and made a few stammering sounds before she could speak.

"I don't have one."

Jordan stroked his nose against her neck again, and then pulled back so he could look into her eyes.

"Everyone has a secret."

Lea thought for a moment and a memory from years before flashed across her mind.

"Well," she said, stroking the hand from the back of his head around to his face to touch his cheek, "Maybe I do. It's nothing like yours, but it is the closest thing I have."

"Tell me."

She smiled at him.

"I have to show you, but I have to change first. Can you meet me back here in an hour?"

Lea was a few minutes early getting back to the bridge, but Jordan was there, sitting on the gravel and leaning back against the same concrete support as she had earlier in the evening. He climbed to his feet when he saw her, his eyes scanning her appreciatively. She felt blatant and exposed in tight black pants and a dark purple shirt that dipped low over her breasts, but she enjoyed the way he seemed to drink her in as she walked closer.

"Is this your secret?"

"There's more. Come with me."

She led him now, letting him walk along beside her as she brought him to her car and drove in silence down city streets that were coming alive in the darkness. A glow in the distance reminded her of part of herself she had locked away, hidden as Brent systematically stripped her of herself.

When they stepped into the nightclub, she felt the familiarity sweep over her, easing the tension in her shoulders and bringing a smile to her lips. The bartender met her eyes and a grin spread across his face. He called her name over the sound of the music and conversations filling the space.

Lea leaned on the edge of the bar so that she could hug Sam.

"Where have you been?" he asked.

She shook her head and looked around, feeling at once like it had been forever since she had been there and like she had never left.

"In another life," she replied, "has it changed in there?"

There was a mischievous glint in Sam's eyes as he shook his head, his attention briefly moving to where Jordan stood close behind her.

"No. Everything is exactly the same. Are you going to dance?"

She shot him a devilish look.

"I just might."

Lea pushed away from the bar and walked through the crowd toward the attached room and the dancefloor. She knew that Jordan followed behind her, watching as those who knew her parted to let her pass. The music pulsed through her as if it filled her blood, speaking to her as if it, too, remembered her. Suddenly she felt Jordan come up to her from behind. His body molded against hers, his hands coming around her to press her back into him.

Without speaking a word, she began to sway against him. His hands gripped her hips as she ground into him and she felt his body begin to move in response to hers. She looped an arm back around his neck and rolled her body against him. Her other hand touched his thigh and slid up until it spread across his hip.

Jordan growled low in his chest and spun her around to face him. Lea's breath caught in her throat as she let him take possession of her, thrusting his leg between hers so that she rode it with each movement of her hips. The friction continued to build the pressure in her belly and she knew he could feel her heat against his thigh. She rolled her hips harder against him and leaned forward so her aching breasts brushed against his chest.

After another song, Jordan led her off of the dancefloor, pushing her backwards toward a black velvet couch away from the crush of dancers. When her thighs touched the couch, he turned her, sitting and pulling her down into his lap so that she straddled his thighs. Lea could feel the other people in the room looking at her, but she didn't care. She concentrated on Jordan's hand as it gently cupped her face, then slid down the front of her neck, between her breasts, and onto her stomach.

She reciprocated by burying her fingers in his hair, drawing them through the thick strands as she stared into the hypnotic blue of his eyes. He pulled her a little closer and she felt his hardness rising up to press against her heat. Lea felt on display, but not in the brutal, unbearable way to which she had become accustomed. Instead, she felt Jordan's protectiveness surrounding her as he touched her, nurturing her with his hands as if to show everyone around them that he was there purely for her and that he would keep her safe.

Jordan reached into his pocket and withdrew a small permanent marker. Removing the cap with his mouth, he took one of her hands from his hair and turned her arm to expose the underside of her wrist. He tucked the end of the marker into the cap so he didn't have to hold it between his teeth anymore and started to draw on her skin.

The feeling of the marker gliding across her skin was intensely erotic and her hips began rocking against him as she watched him draw a smooth, complex design onto her. She whimpered, aching for him to touch her, craving the feeling of his mouth on hers.

"My original tag," he said as quietly as he could while still ensuring she could hear his voice over the music. "I haven't drawn it in two years."

Their eyes met and Jordan tucked a hand around the back of her head, bringing her forward so he could capture her mouth with his. She moaned into the kiss, opening her mouth and welcoming his tongue as it slipped past her lips to touch hers. He kissed her deeply but without aggression and her body relaxed in his hold. Jordan's mouth moved slowly over hers, exploring with his tongue and occasionally lifting away to suck lightly on her bottom lip or offer a softer, lighter kiss.

"Lea," Sam's voice teased from behind her and Lea took her mouth reluctantly from Jordan's so she could look over her shoulder at her friend, "I thought you said you were going to dance."

He extended a hand and Lea glanced at Jordan. His desire-darkened eyes stared back at her questioningly and a smile curved her lips.

"Are you ready for my secret?" she asked coyly.

"This wasn't your secret?" he asked with a laugh.

"Oh, Honey, you don't know Lea as I would like to think you do after seeing that kiss," Sam said, then turned his attention back to Lea. "Shall we show him why you are so famous around here?"

Lea gave Jordan another brief kiss before letting Sam help her off of his lap and guide her across the dancefloor toward one of the large steel cages that stood on platforms in front of the DJ booth. She stepped into the cage and let Sam close the door behind her. Across the room she saw shock register on Jordan's face and it filled her with a thrill and sense of empowerment she had not felt in a long time.

The music changed and she began to dance, immediately drawing the attention of everyone around her. They stopped to watch her, cheering up at her, the ones who remembered her calling her name. Lea felt herself smiling, finally feeling open and free again.

Suddenly there was a scream and the clang of something hitting the bars of the cage made Lea jump and turn around. She saw Jordan pushing through the crowd to get across the dancefloor before she saw Brent climbing gripping the door. When she did see Brent, she gasped, stumbling back against the opposite wall of the cage.

"I told you never to get in this cage again," he snarled at her.

"What are you doing here?" she asked desperately.

"I'm on bail, thanks to you, and I thought I might find you here. Get out of there, now. I told you that no girl of mine would ever parade herself like a fucking whore in a cage."

"I'm not your girl, Brent, and I am just dancing."

There was a quiver in her voice, but Lea felt stronger with each word. She reached up to grip the bar above her head with one hand and saw Brent's eyes flash with anger.

"What the hell is that?"

She looked at her arm and saw Jordan's tag gleaming against her skin, for the first time realizing that it covered the bruises that Brent had left. Her hand released the bar and she strode forward just as Jordan made it to the platform and reached up to tear Brent down into the crowd. He tossed him to the ground and stepped on his chest to hold him down.

"I told you to stay away from her," he shouted and he pulled back to punch him, but Lea called out to stop him.

Opening the door to the cage, she slowly descended the stairs of the platform, knowing Jordan would not let him off the floor. She stared down at Brent lying beneath her and felt a sudden wave of pity. Positioning herself so she was close to Jordan but still on her own, Lea crouched down beside Brent. She reached forward and Brent pulled back.

"Don't worry," she said calmly, "I'm not going to hit you. I don't need to." She pushed a piece of hair away from his forehead, and then pulled her hand back." You don't have that power over me anymore."

Lea stood and met Jordan's eyes. He shoved his foot one final time deep into Brent's ribs, and then stepped away from him. Brent stood and looked between them, and then rushed away, forcing his way through the crowd toward the door. The other people in the club around her erupted in cheers, but she couldn't hear anything but the blood rushing in her ears and the pounding of her own heartbeat.

Jordan's voice came at her as if through water, saying her name, calling out to her. She saw his hand reach for her, then darkness came as her body gave out. The darkness lasted only a moment before she felt herself swept into Jordan's arms. He cradled her against his chest and pushed his way to the door as she clung to him, giving herself over to the protection of his arms, his body, and the sound of his heartbeat joining hers.

Chapter 6: Washed Clean

A summer thunderstorm rolled in while they were inside the club and Lea felt the curtain of rain pouring down on her as soon as Jordan stepped outside. He didn't put her down, walking through the soothing drops toward her car. She looked up at him and saw rain streaming from his hair and clinging to his eyelashes like tears.

When they got to the car, Jordan held her with one arm so he could open the passenger door and place her gently inside. She had already given him her keys to carry since she did not have pockets and he climbed behind the wheel.

"Where do you live?" he asked pointedly.

Lea forced her address out of her mouth then fell silent again. She was unsure of the emotions that rolled through her like the thunder that echoed above, but the one she felt the strongest was relief.

Jordan drove to her apartment, parked, and came around to help her out of the car. He led her to the door and let them both in. After roaming through the apartment like a guard dog, he brushed a wet lock of hair out of her eyes and suggested she take a shower. The idea of a hot shower sounded blissful and she agreed immediately, telling him to make himself at home as she dragged herself into the bathroom.

She peeled off her soaked clothing, letting each piece fall to the tile as she enjoyed a brief moment of the air conditioning cooling her bare skin. The shower seemed loud in the small room, but she reveled in the dependable, soothing sound. Lea stepped beneath the stream of water so hot that it stung as it touched her and let it stream over her body. Her head fell back, allowing the water to flow down her breasts and onto her stomach.

Filling her hands with soap she lathered her skin and her hair, letting the sweet smell envelope her as the hot water washed away the sweat, the anger, the pain, and the past. She laughed up into the stream, emotion bubbling out of her. The hot liquid slipping past her lips and into her throat made her stomach clench and she swallowed, closing her eyes to fully savor the fantasy that sensation brought to mind.

As if her thoughts had lured him, she watched through the frosted glass shower door as Jordan stepped into the bathroom. She could only see his form through the hazy glass, and the obscured detail tormented her as he removed his shirt and tossed it aside. He was watching her as intently as she was watching him and Lea let her hands continue sliding across her body, tempting him with the curves he could see through the glass.

Jordan's hands moved to his belt and he released it quickly, kicking his pants aside when they fell to his feet. She bit her bottom lip as he pushed his trunks down from his hips and let them join his pants.

He didn't immediately climb in with her, but stood just on the other side of the glass, continuing to watch her. Lea pressed her hand to the glass and he reciprocated, aligning his palm with hers and stretching his fingers along where hers spread against the door. A moment later, he slid the door aside and stepped in.

Lea stepped forward to meet him and their mouths came together, already open, seeking one another. She let her eyes close and let the kiss consume her. Jordan's hands moved over her with confidence and she relinquished herself to his power. Leaning forward, she touched her wet, naked body against his, coaxing him to step under the water with her. He groaned and kissed her more deeply, responding to the touch of her body by taking her hips in his hands and pulling her against him roughly.

The sudden movement made Lea gasp and she looked into his eyes hungrily. Jordan applied pressure to her hips until she turned in his hands and he could draw her back against him. She felt his erection pressing into her lower back and she groaned, arching to feel it more fully on her skin. Her hand slid up his outer thigh, coming between them, but he eased it away before she could touch him. When she moaned in protest, Jordan dropped his mouth to her neck, trailing kisses up to her ear so he could whisper to her.

"Not yet."

"Why?" she whispered back, her voice high with desire.

"You, first."

"What?"

Jordan rubbed the hard length of his shaft against her, eliciting a whimper.

"I have wanted to fuck you since you showed up in that alley a few days ago." Lea gasped at his words, but Jordan continued, "And I am going to, if you want me to." Lea murmured an affirmation and felt his lips smile against her ear, "But before I do, I am going to show you how you should be touched."

"Jordan," she sighed and felt his hand slide against her waist around to the front of her belly.

"I am going to touch you." His hand applied pressure to her belly and slid down, dipping into her folds as he whispered. Lea cried out at the delicious sensation of his finger stroking her slowly, patiently coaxing her forward. "I am going to lick you, and I am going to make you come. Then I am going to leave you here." Lea shook her head frantically, her hips rolling against his hand even as she tried to protest what he said. "Shhhh. Don't worry. I'm only going as far as your bedroom. You will stay here and think."

"About what?" Lea panted.

Jordan responded by slipping his hand down further and pressing inside her, adding a second finger to the first and supporting her with his other arm as she arched against him.

"About me. Think about how I made you feel. Think about my hands and my mouth on you. Then think about whether you want me inside you. If you decide that you do, come tell me and I will very happily fuck you until you can barely remember your own name. But trust me," he gently bit her earlobe and Lea sagged against him, "you'll remember mine."

Chapter 7: Surrender

Jordan withdrew his fingers from Lea's body and she felt him take a step back so that they came out from under the water. He held her tightly against him and slid down the shower wall, lowering them to the floor. The water rained down on her, teasing across her nipples and pooling at the apex of her thighs where she pressed her legs together.

"Relax," he said, carefully easing her legs apart and draping them over his on either side of her.

The position made the water stream down her most sensitive areas, making her writhe against him. His fingers continued their exploration of her, tenderly swirling into her wet heat and stroking the swollen bud his patience revealed. When she was whimpering in his arms he ducked his head to her ear again.

"Turn around."

Lea complied willingly, feeling delightfully, happily powerless under his touch. She pulled her legs off of his, folded them in, and turned to face him. Jordan reached behind her to turn off the faucet, then brought a kiss to her lips. When he took his mouth from hers he used his hands on her hips to push her as far back in the tub as she could go. She felt him get on his knees between her legs and slip his hands under her to guide her into a reclining position and tilt her pelvis up to him.

She gasped loudly as his mouth touched her, his tongue masterfully repeating the movements of his hand. He lifted her legs to rest on his shoulders and lifted her hips higher, delving his tongue deeply inside her. She tightened her muscles, part of her fighting against the waves of pleasure descending on her as they threatened to overwhelm her.

Jordan took his mouth from her and looked up at her. His eyes were so startlingly beautiful she felt held in place by them.

"Relax," he repeated. "Let me get you there. Trust me."

With that, Lea let her eyes drift close and relaxed into his hands. Jordan's tongue returned to her, flicking over her sensitive pearl, then taking a long, slow dip all the way back inside her. The pressure intensified in her pelvis and she resisted the urge to buck against his mouth. She whimpered his name and he responded by opening his mouth over her, sucking her peak in against his tongue.

That sensation pushed her over the edge and Lea screamed as her entire body contracted, and then released her into an all-consuming, tremoring orgasm. Jordan gave a final, gentle lick then eased her legs off of his shoulders, pushing forward to hover over her. He nuzzled his nose with hers, then kissed her, nipping at her bottom lip.

Without another word, he climbed out of the shower and grabbed a towel off of the stack on her shelf as he walked out of the bathroom. Just as he had said, he left her alone with her thoughts. Lea lay shuddering on the bottom of the tub, her heart pounding so hard she had to fight to catch her breath. She closed her eyes again, letting the last tremors roll through her.

As he had asked, she thought about Jordan carefully. She thought about the strength of his hands on her body and the new, exquisite feeling of his tongue worshipping her. Just the memory of his completely selfless attention had her writhing with desire again, but the reality of him waiting for her in her bedroom was somewhat daunting. She worried about letting him so close, allowing herself to draw that near to him.

The cold around her made her open her eyes and stand, and as she reached for a towel she caught a glimpse of the ink on her arm. She turned her wrist over and examined the tag. The black ink stretched across the bruise as if shielding her from looking at it. By tagging her, Jordan had claimed her, literally placing himself between her and the last lingering remnants of Brent. It was his silent promise of protection and respect.

Lea climbed out of the tub and dried herself thoroughly, not bothering to wrap herself with the towel. Instead, she walked completely bare down the hall and into her bedroom. Jordan had not turned on the light and instead sat on the bed in a pool of illumination from the streetlamp outside. Propped against the headboard he gently stroked his staff, staring her directly in the eyes as she approached the bed.

Having no words in that moment, she got on her knees on the end of the bed and crawled toward him. She used one hand to move his hand from his cock and drew her tongue along its underside up to the head, using the tip to trace around his crown. Jordan drew a sharp breath in between his teeth and she opened her mouth to take him in fully. Lying on her side between his legs, Lea sucked him passionately, drawing him deeper with each stroke of her mouth.

A few moments later Jordan grabbed the base of his erection and carefully eased it out of her mouth.

"You are going to make me come," he panted, "Which is fine if that is what you want."

Lea shook her head and repositioned herself so she was on her knees.

"No. That's not what I want," she answered, her voice growing stronger as she spoke.

Jordan sat up and drew his legs in so he could mimic her position, kneeling in the center of the bed so that their bodies touched.

"What do you want, Lea?" he asked, resting his forehead against hers and intertwining their fingers beside him.

The moment was tender, but it didn't lessen the purely erotic effect his body had on her. Crafted for sin and embedded with ink, it was the subject of every fantasy she could conjure in her mind, and she wanted to explore each and every one with him.

"Tell me what you want," Jordan urged again, inching forward to press more firmly against her.

"I want you to fuck me," she whispered and felt his erection jump in response.

Jordan's mouth crushed down on hers and she kissed him back with all of the intensity he had so carefully and patiently withheld until now. Using his strong hands to guide her down onto the bed, he pulled her legs up around his waist and plunged inside her. He felt even bigger inside her than he had looked and Lea arched off the bed as he filled her. She felt him brace himself on either side of her and hold himself still, pushed so deeply inside her she felt like she could not handle anymore. A sob of pleasure escaped her lips and she rested down onto the mattress.

As soon as he body relaxed, Jordan's hips started to move. He rolled them into her, stroking her with a rhythm that brought a series of tiny, gasping cries from her throat. Her eyes closed and he immediately leaned down to kiss her.

"Open your eyes. Look at me," he whispered to her.

Lea met his gaze and his pace increased. She released her legs from around his waist and brought them down so just the tips of her pointed toes touched the mattress. This sent him even deeper and Jordan groaned, thrusting harder and faster into her body. He brought chest forward to close the space between them and she felt their skin slipping across each other with water and sweat.

Lea dug her fingernails into his back, scratching from his shoulder blades to his hips, then grabbing onto his butt to follow his rocking. His sounds became low and rhythmic as the wonderful, dizzying pressure began to build again inside Lea. Suddenly she crashed into another hard, powerful orgasm and tossed her head back to scream his name. This seemed to remove his final grasp of control and he gave one more forceful, impaling thrust and roared as his climax consumed him.

Lea's tremors milked him and she felt his cock throb inside her as he poured into her.

Jordan collapsed onto her, kissing her as she wrapped her arms around him. She held him inside her, relishing the feeling of this primal bad boy shuddering and sweaty against her. Her eyes closed and she drifted to sleep. She knew that tomorrow he would help her more with her project and she would offer him support and encouragement. When the story came out, he would come with her as she explored the country and chronicled more of the street art that had captured her interest, and now her heart. With each kiss, each touch, each word they would put their pasts further behind them and walk into the future, together.

My Other Books and Audio Books

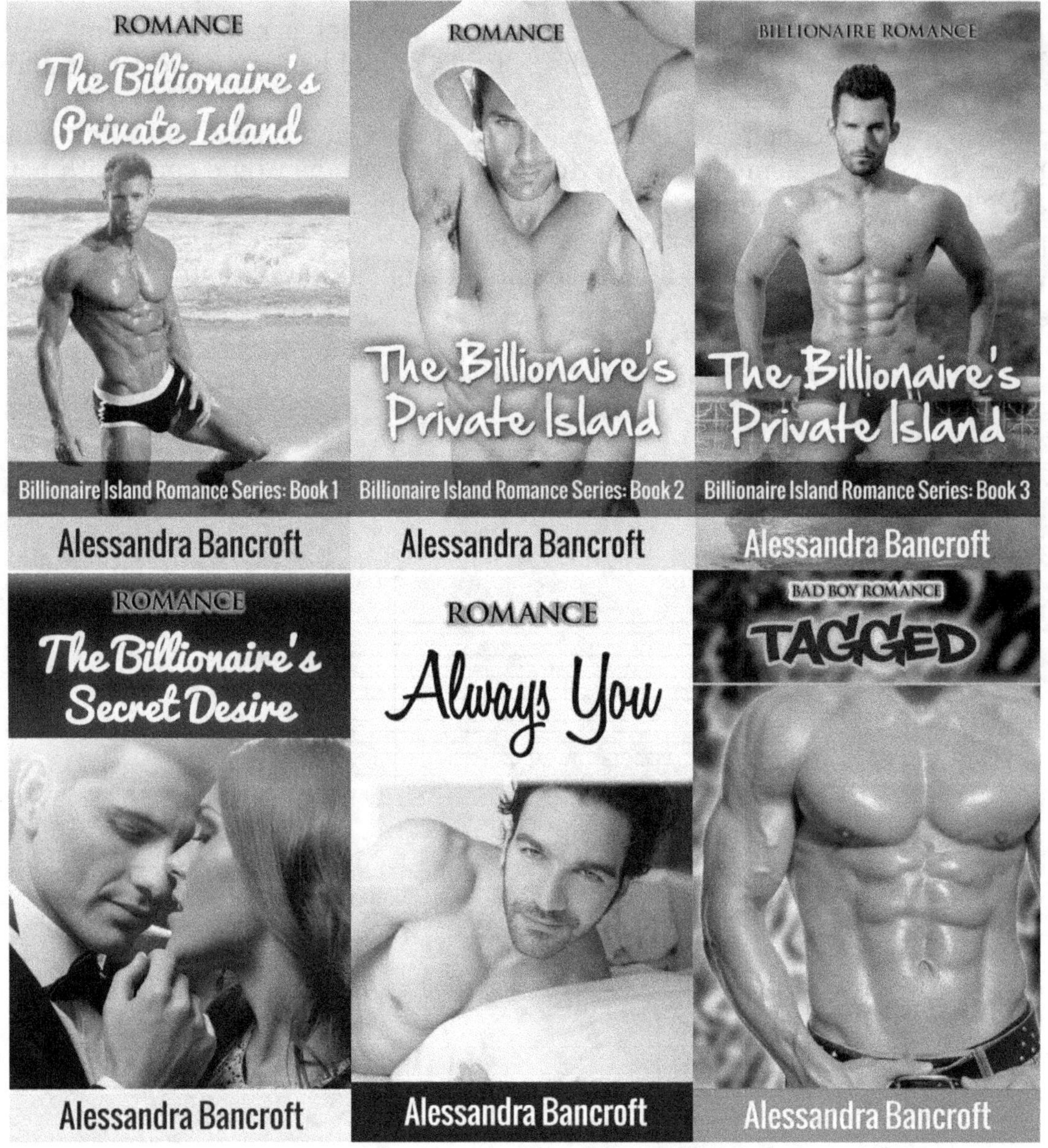

All of these are available in audio book as well.

If you enjoyed this book then please spare a few seconds to easily post a quick positive review. It would be greatly appreciated!

Thanks for reading.